PINKY and REX
and the
School Play

OTHER ALADDIN PAPERBACKS BY JAMES HOWE

PINKY and REX
and the
School Play

by James Howe
illustrated by Melissa Sweet

Ready-to-Read

Simon Spotlight

Simon Spotlight
An imprint of Simon & Schuster Children's Publishing Division
1230 Avenue of the Americas
New York, New York 10020

Book design by Michael Nelson

The text of this book is set in Utopia.
The illustrations are rendered in watercolor.

First Aladdin Paperbacks Edition, 1998

Printed in the United States of America

17 19 20 18 16

The Library of Congress has cataloged the Atheneum Books for Young Readers Edition
as follows:
Howe, James, 1946–
Pinky and Rex and the school play / by James Howe ;
illustrated by Melissa Sweet.—1st Aladdin Paperbacks ed.
p. cm.
Summary: Pinky is jealous when his best friend Rex gets the lead in the school play,
even though she only tried out to give Pinky moral support.
[1. Plays—Fiction. 2. Jealousy—Fiction. 3. Schools—Fiction. 4. Friendship—Fiction.]
I. Sweet, Melissa, ill. II. Title.
PZ7.H83727Pip   1998
[E]—dc21
97-732
CIP   AC
ISBN-13: 978-0-689-31872-6   ISBN-10: 0-689-31872-3 (hc.)
ISBN-13: 978-0-689-81704-5   ISBN-10: 0-689-81704-5 (pbk.)
0815 LAK

To my friend, Philip Marchand
—J. H.

To my friend Jim, and to all of his students at
the Miller School
—M. S.

Contents

Chapter 1
Davi, Boy of the Rain Forest

Pinky drained his carton of milk with a noisy slurp, then glanced up at the cafeteria clock. Only five minutes to go.

"What are you so nervous about?" Rex asked from across the table.

"What makes you think I'm nervous?"

"Come on, Pinky. That was your third carton of milk. When you're this thirsty, it means you're nervous. There isn't a test this afternoon, is there?" She looked up from her cheese sandwich. "*Is* there?"

Pinky shook his head. "No, but there are tryouts for the school play, don't you remember?"

Rex shrugged.

"*Davi, Boy of the Rain Forest.* I've

been practicing for the part of Davi all week. Want to hear a secret, Rex? I'm going to be an actor when I grow up."

"You are?" Rex was surprised to find out her best friend had a secret she'd never heard before.

Pinky nodded. "Yep. Maybe I'll even be famous. You're going to try out, too, aren't you?"

Rex smirked. "No way," she said, checking her lunch box to see if there was a note from her mom. Her mom always used to put little notes in Rex's lunch box. They said things like "I love you" or "Good luck on your test today." But ever since her baby brother had arrived, her mother kept forgetting— except for last week, when she put one in by mistake that read, "Diaper service. Babysitter. Strained beets."

There was no note this time, not even a wrong one. Rex sighed and looked at Pinky, who was eyeing her milk carton. "You wouldn't get *me* up on a stage in front of all those people," she said. "I'd forget what I was supposed to say and make a total fool of myself."

"Maybe you'd get a part with no words," Pinky said.

"Then I'd forget what I was supposed to do."

The bell rang. Rex grabbed her milk carton, then handed it to Pinky. She didn't know how he could still look thirsty, but he did.

Pinky drank it down in one gulp. "Would you come to the tryouts to keep me company?" he asked, wiping away his milk mustache with the back of his hand. Rex shook her head. "Ple-e-ease!

If you come you'll get out of spelling!"

Rex's head stopped shaking.

"Honest? Well . . . okay. Just to keep you company."

Pinky smiled. "With you there," he said, "I *know* I'll get the part!"

Chapter 2

Pinky's Part

"A monkey?"

Pinky couldn't believe his eyes. It had been two days since the tryouts, and the cast list had just gone up on the bulletin board outside the main office. There under "Monkeys" were six names. One of them was his. He kept closing his eyes and opening them again.

It didn't go away. He was a monkey. Nowhere did he see the name of "Davi."

"I don't get it," he said as his classmate Anthony came up behind him and looked over his shoulder.

"Weird," Anthony said.

"What's weird?"

"Up until Mr. Lacey had the tryouts, the play was called *Davi, Boy of the Rain Forest.* Now look what it's called."

Pinky looked at the top of the sheet of paper. "Cast List for *Bahi, Girl of the Rain Forest,*" it read. So that was why Pinky hadn't seen the name "Davi." In its place on the list of characters was "Bahi," and opposite the name of Bahi was another name. Pinky's jaw dropped.

"Rex."

He opened and closed his eyes again and again to make sure he was seeing

right. Rex had gotten the part he wanted.
Or the part he had wanted when it was
a boy's part. And she hadn't even wanted
to be in the play. She'd only tried out
to get out of spelling!

Pinky turned and glared at Anthony
as if this mess were all his fault. Anthony
smiled. "You'll make a good monkey,"
he said. "You like bananas."

Later in class, Pinky wouldn't even
look at Rex.

"I'm never going to speak to you
again," he told her when she tried to join
him walking home. "You're supposed
to be my friend!"

"I am your friend," Rex said. "Stop

walking so fast! And anyway, it was
your idea for me to go with you to the
tryouts. I don't even want to be in the
play. What if I throw up?"

Pinky stopped in his tracks. "Yeah,"
he said, "that would be terrible. I think
you should tell Mr. Lacey—"

"On the other hand," Rex said, "Mr. Lacey told me I was so good he was changing the main character to a girl. I guess he should know what he's talking about."

Pinky's lips got very tight. "It's a good thing I don't have a speaking part," he spat out.

"Why?" Rex asked.

"Because *I'm never going to speak to you again!*"

He stormed away so fast a book fell out of his backpack. Rex picked it up and looked at the title: *So You Want to Be an Actor.* She shook her head. Poor Pinky.

Chapter 3

Rehearsals

Mr. Lacey stood at the back of the auditorium, his hands cupped around his mouth like a megaphone.

"Can't hear you, Rex!" he called out.

Huddled with the other monkeys onstage, Pinky saw Rex's cheeks turn red. "If I say it any louder," she mumbled, "my eyeballs will pop out of

my head and roll off the stage." Some kids laughed, but Pinky could see Rex was embarrassed. He would have felt sorry for her if she was still his friend.

Ever since rehearsals had started two weeks ago, he had done everything he could to avoid her. Once she called him on the phone and told him he deserved to be a monkey because he was acting like one. But he *didn't* deserve it. Stephanie Birch deserved to be a monkey; she was always scratching herself anyway. And Tommy McKay *looked* like a monkey. But Pinky wanted to be the star, not jump around the stage dangling his arms and screeching. It wasn't fair.

"Hurry, hurry!" Rex shouted. "Run to the *maloca,* before it is too late!"

"Much better, Rex! I could hear every word." Mr. Lacey walked back down the aisle to the stage as he called out his directions. "Now, everyone—no, monkeys, not you, just *people* . . ." (Pinky rolled his eyes) " . . . run to the *maloca,* that's the big house, stage left."

As Pinky watched Rex lead the other children away, Stephanie Birch's elbow jabbed his ribs. He turned. She was scratching under her arm.

"We don't have to act now," he told her.

"I'm not acting," she replied.

Pinky wondered if she really had fleas.

Most of the rehearsals were the same. Rex got to say things and run around the stage. Pinky got to sit under cardboard trees and have his ribs

16

jabbed by Stephanie Birch's elbow. Still, he went to every rehearsal and listened to every word Mr. Lacey said. He had decided that even if he was only a monkey this time he was going to be a great actor someday, and he had a lot to learn.

Chapter 4

Punky the Monkey

"What's your name in the play?" Pinky's little sister Amanda asked at dinner. It was the night before the big performance. Pinky was nervous. He had already had two glasses of water.

"I don't have a name," he said. "I'm just a monkey."

"I've got one for you," Amanda said,

chomping a carrot stick. "You could change your name from Pinky to Punky. Get it? Punky the Monkey!"

"Amanda the Panda," said Pinky, not laughing.

"Cut it out, you two," their father said. "Amanda, don't make fun of your brother. He's worked very hard on this play."

"Why?" Amanda asked. "He's only a monkey."

Pinky could feel a lump growing in his throat. "May I be excused?" he asked. "I don't feel like eating."

"Sure," his mother said. "Maybe you'll be hungry later."

Pinky started up the stairs to his bedroom, then changed his mind and went out the front door. He sat down on the stoop and tried to swallow the lump. Tomorrow was going to be the worst day of his life. It was bad enough he had to be a monkey, but his mother had made his costume out of a leftover Halloween cat costume. It was gray. All the other monkeys were brown. He was a gray cat pretending to be a brown monkey.

"Hi."

Pinky looked up in surprise. Rex was standing at the end of his sidewalk.

"Oh, hi," he said softly.

"I, uh, I've had this in my room for the past couple of weeks. I keep forgetting to give it to you." She walked up to him and handed him the book that had fallen out of his backpack—*So You Want to Be an Actor.* Pinky looked at it and snorted.

"You can keep it," he said.

Rex shook her head. "You're the one who wants to be an actor."

"Yeah, but you're the one who *is* the actor."

"I don't care about it the way you do, Pinky. It's been fun, but like my mom says, it's only a play. And it'll be over tomorrow. Are you still going to be mad at me after that?"

Pinky shook his head.

"Good," Rex said. "Then we can be friends again."

Pinky looked at the book in his hands. He still wished he was playing the big part in the play tomorrow, but Rex's mom was right. It *was* only a play. Besides, it wasn't Rex's fault he was a monkey. It really didn't make sense that he'd been mad at her all this time.

"We can be friends again now," he said. He paused and added, "If you want to be." Rex nodded. The two friends smiled at each other.

Then Pinky looked back at the book in his hands. "There's something I wanted to tell you," he said. "You're really good in the play."

"Thanks," Rex said. "But I'm still worried I'm going to throw up."

Chapter 5

Show Time!

The auditorium was buzzing.

"There must be a million people out there," Stephanie Birch said.

"*Two* million," said Tommy McKay, peeking through the break in the curtain, after Mr. Lacey had told everyone at least ten times not to peek through the break in the curtain and not to wave and say, "Hi, Mom!"

"Hi, Mom!" Pinky heard Tommy McKay shout.

"Hi, Pinky, are you all set?" Pinky looked up at the sound of Mr. Lacey's voice. "Your parents did a great job on that costume," the director went on. "I'm glad not all the monkeys are brown. That would be pretty boring, don't you think?" Pinky shrugged. "Besides, this way you'll stand out from the crowd."

Pinky hadn't thought about that. "Yeah," he said. "That's why my mom did it. I guess."

Mr. Lacey smiled. He had a great smile. Pinky couldn't help smiling back. "Break a leg," the director said.

"Huh?"

"It's a theater expression. It means 'good luck.'"

"Oh. Thanks."

Mr. Lacey asked his assistant, a fifth-grader named Sara, to call everybody together onstage. The show was going to start in five minutes!

Pinky found Rex in the crowd. "I'm so thirsty," he told her. "But if I get a drink of water now, I'll have to pee in the middle of the play."

"I'm going to throw up," said Rex.

They looked at each other and laughed. "Break a leg," Pinky whispered as Sara held up two fingers, indicating that everyone should be quiet.

"You, too," Rex whispered back. Pinky made a monkey face and scratched his armpits.

Mr. Lacey thanked all the children for their hard work, and reminded them to talk in a big voice (he glanced at Rex) and *not* to look out at the audience. Then he said, "Show time!" and five kids raised their hands to ask if they could go to the bathroom.

Pinky could hardly believe it when the play actually began. He knew he wasn't supposed to, but he kept looking out from behind his makeup to find where his family was sitting. He didn't think

anybody noticed until he heard Amanda
yell, "Over here, Pinky!" From that
moment on, he kept his eyes onstage.

The play was going much faster than
it had in rehearsal. Pinky was having fun.

He thought he even heard people
laughing when he ran away with one
of the other monkey's bananas. Rex
seemed to be having a good time, too.
And she was talking in her biggest voice.

"Hurry, hurry!" she shouted. "Run to the *maloca,* before it is too late!"

Pinky sat with his fellow monkeys under the cardboard tree waiting for the other children to run to the big house. But something was wrong. No one was moving. Pinky could see Mr. Lacey backstage motioning with his hands for everyone to stand up, but no one else saw him.

Rex looked at Pinky with wide eyes that asked, *What do I do now?* Pinky shrugged helplessly. The audience began to cough and whisper.

Suddenly, Pinky had an idea.

Jumping up so fast he almost knocked over the cardboard tree, he began hopping around the stage, going from one group of children to the next.

"Stand up! Stand up!" he hissed in the children's ears. In between groups, he screeched and scratched, and the audience laughed at the funny monkey. And the children all stood up.

Rex shouted, "Hurry! Run to the

maloca, before it is too late!"

Everyone ran and the audience broke into applause.

Pinky returned to his tree. When he looked backstage, he could see Mr. Lacey smiling right at him.

Chapter 6

A Surprise for Pinky

"You were the best monkey,"
Amanda said, running up to Pinky
after the show. "Even if you did look
like a—"

"You were wonderful," his mother
said, before Amanda could say "cat."

"And it looked to me like you saved
the show at one point," said his father.

"He sure did." Pinky recognized the director's voice. After introducing himself to Pinky's parents, Mr. Lacey said, "Your son paid careful attention to everything I said in rehearsals, even though he had only a small part. I'll bet he could have saved the show at *any* point."

Just then, Rex and her family came over.

"Oh, Rex!" Amanda cried. "You were so-o-o good. Are you going to be a movie star when you grow up?"

"No way," said Rex. "I'm through with acting."

"That's too bad," her father said. "You *were* very good."

"I can be good at something and not have to want to do it, can't I?" Rex asked. Her father looked surprised, but nodded his head. "It's just that there's other stuff I'd rather do, like soccer."

Amanda thought Rex was crazy not to want to be a movie star.

"Join us for an ice cream celebration?" Pinky's father asked Mr. Lacey.

"I'd love to," the director said. "Let me get my jacket."

When he returned, he pulled something

out of his pocket. "I got this out of the
library for you yesterday, Pinky. I thought
it might interest you."

Pinky looked at the book Mr. Lacey
handed him: *How to Put on a Play*. "I
think you have the makings of a director.
In fact, I was wondering if you'd like to
be my assistant on the next school play."

"Really?" Pinky said. "But I thought
you had to be in fifth grade."

Mr. Lacey shook his head. "You just have to have the interest," he told Pinky. "And the talent."

Pinky beamed. "Thanks," he said.

"Race you to the ice cream store," said Rex.

When they got there, everyone made jokes about whether to order the Rain Forest Crumble or a banana split. In the end, Pinky ordered a hot fudge sundae with extra whipped cream. So did Rex.

Because sometimes best friends just have to have the same thing.